# Country Bear's Good Neighbor

# Country Bear's
# Good Neighbor

By Larry Dane Brimner
Illustrations by Ruth Tietjen Councell

Orchard Books
*A division of Franklin Watts*
New York

Orchard Books
387 Park Avenue South, New York, New York 10016

Orchard Books Great Britain
10 Golden Square, London W1R 3AF England

Orchard Books Australia
14 Mars Road, Lane Cove, New South Wales 2066

Orchard Books Canada
20 Torbay Road, Markham, Ontario 23P 1G6

Orchard Books is a division of Franklin Watts, Inc.

The text of this book is set in 18 point Cochin.
The illustrations are colored pencil drawings.
Manufactured in the United States of America.
Book design by Sylvia Frezzolini.

10  9  8  7  6  5  4  3  2  1

Library of Congress Cataloging-in-Publication Data
Brimner, Larry Dane.   Country Bear's good neighbor.
Summary: Country Bear borrows all the ingredients for a cake from his neighbor and then gives
her the cake as a present. [1. Neighborliness – Fiction.   2. Borrowing and lending – Fiction.
3. Bears – Fiction]   I. Councell, Ruth Tietjen, ill.   II. Title.   PZ7.B767Co   1987
[E]    87-5704        ISBN 0-531-05708-9        ISBN 0-531-08308-X (lib. bdg.)

*For Pam Brimner O'Karma*
L. D. B.

*For my father*
R. T. C.

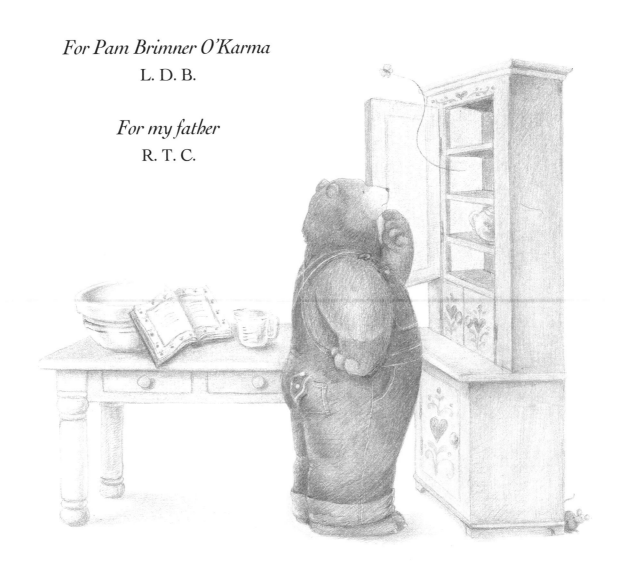

Good morning, Country Bear.
What's in the bowl?

You want to borrow some apples?
Certainly!
That's what good neighbors are for.

Country Bear, have you
come back to visit?

Oh.
You thought you had some sugar,
but you cannot find any.
Just a minute, Country Bear.
That's what good neighbors are for.

Back again, Country Bear?
An egg?

Yes, Country Bear.
I think I have an egg.

Now what, Country Bear?
Flour and walnuts?
Cinnamon and butter?

Is there anything else?

You are lucky
I am a good neighbor,
Country Bear.

Absolutely not!
Don't even ask, Country Bear!
You have my apples.
My sugar.
My flour.
My walnuts.
My cinnamon.
The butter.
The milk.
AND
the only egg.

Oh? For me?
Why,
thank you.

Now come and share it
Country Bear.
That's what good
neighbors are for.

# Country Bear's Good Neighbor Cake

4 cups apples, peeled
  and thinly sliced
½ cup sugar
1 teaspoon cinnamon
½ cup chopped walnuts
1 cup flour
¾ cup sugar

¾ teaspoon baking powder
¼ teaspoon salt
1 egg, well-beaten
3 teaspoon water
⅓ cup evaporated milk
½ cup melted butter,
  cooled

*equipment*
1 9-inch round baking dish
2 mixing bowls

Preheat oven to 325°.
Place apples in a 9-inch round, well-buttered
baking dish. Sprinkle ½ cup sugar and cinnamon
over the apples. Next sprinkle the walnuts over
the apples. In a mixing bowl, sift together
the flour, ¾ cup sugar, baking powder,
and salt. Set it aside. In another bowl,
combine the egg, water, evaporated milk, and
melted butter. Add the egg mixture all at once
to the flour mixture. Mix until smooth. Pour
the batter over the apples. Bake for about
1 hour (or until golden) in a 325°F. oven.
Enjoy Country Bear's Good Neighbor Cake
with a friend.